Melody and the bouncing shoes

Written by Mandy Shade
Illustrations by Juliette Bacuvier

Bumblebee Books
London

BUMBLEBEE PAPERBACK EDITION

Illustrations by Juliette Bacuvier

A CIP catalogue record for this title is
available from the British Library.

ISBN: 978-1-83934-430-5

Bumblebee Books is an imprint of
Olympia Publishers.

First Published in 2021

Bumblebee Books
Tallis House
2 Tallis Street
London
EC4Y 0AB

Printed in Great Britain

www.olympiapublishers.com

Dedication

I dedicate this book to my children, Lucy, Jessica and Oliver.
Mummy loves you XX

This is Melody with her long curly hair, bright blue eyes and the biggest frown you ***ever*** saw.
You see, Melody wasn't like the other mermaids. Her tail didn't swish and sway like the others.

She could never keep up with their swimming and they always laughed at her because of it.

"Melody, you're sooo slow!" they would tease, before swimming away.

Melody hated that she was different. None of the other mermaids liked her. They would whisper whenever she was around and giggle at how slow she was.

Her only real friend was Rex, the seahorse. He was blue and yellow, and Melody thought he was beautiful. He was also kind and that was why they were friends. Rex didn't mind how fast she swam as long as they were having fun.

Melody spent a lot of her time at the pier watching humans walking past.

Why, I hear you ask?

Because she absolutely

LOVED shoes!

She spent all
of her time
snapping pictures
of high ones, flat
ones, sporty ones
and her most
favourite of all...
sparkly ones.

Her bedroom wall was covered with all her favourites.
It was the only thing that truly made her happy.

One day, Melody woke with a great idea.

"Maybe I can make my own shoes like the people at the pier. Then I'll be the envy of all the other mermaids."

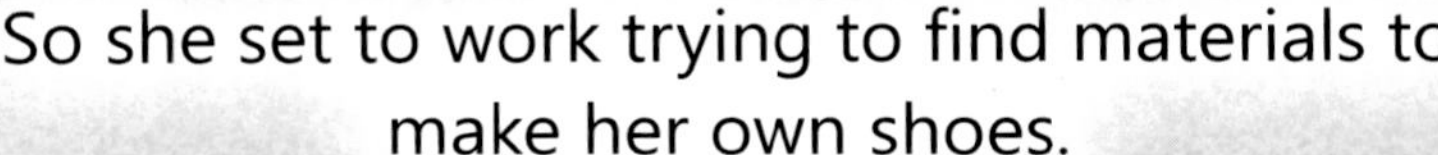

So she set to work trying to find materials to make her own shoes.

It took her a while, but then Melody found some beautiful shells.

"These are perfect," she screamed in delight.

She set to work, adding jewels to make them sparkle. Melody couldn't wait to show Rex.

She worked long hours of the night to have them ready for the next day and by the end of it, she had the most beautiful pair of sparkling shell-shoes.

The next morning, Melody proudly swam to see Rex. The other mermaids watched her, curious about the shell-shoes she was wearing on the tip of her tail.

"Rex!" she called to him.

Rex swam over.

"Wow, Melody. What's that on your tail?"

"My shell-shoes," she said with a smile. "Look, watch."

She swished her tail to plant her shoes on the ocean floor,

but as soon as she stood up on them,

they cracked under her weight, leaving her poor tail cut and bruised.

The other mermaids laughed loudly and swam off, leaving Melody red-faced and moaning as the pain went through her tail.

Rex quickly swam to
her side.
"Are you OK?" he said.
"They are beautiful
shoes, Melody, I'm sorry they broke."
"It's OK," Melody said, turning away so he wouldn't see
the tears in her eyes.

Melody was determined to try again. This time she was on the hunt for something soft.
What did she find?

Some bright,
green seaweed!

"Perfect!" she beamed.
She got to work on the shoes,
adding rainbow ribbons and
glitter to make them extra special.
"These look amazing, I can't wait,"
Melody squealed.
BUT...

When the time came to show them the next day, they were sooo slippery.

As she planted them on the ocean floor again, poor Melody went flying right in front of all the other mermaids.

Everyone laughed.

"It's no use!" cried Melody, as they all swam away, their laughter filling the sea. "It'll never work!"

Rex gave Melody a cuddle.

"You can do anything you set your mind to," he said. "I know you feel sad, but if you work hard, you can achieve anything. Come on, show me that smile."

As he hugged her, Melody watched his bouncy tail bopping in the sea.

Then an idea struck her.

“That’s it,” shouted Melody suddenly. “I’ve got it!”

She swam off to the shore to find new materials. This new idea was going to be great – and she knew it would work this time!

She found some jellyfish washed up on the shore and had a quick chat with them. Then she took them back home to begin her work.

Melody stayed up all night designing her new shoes. Sewing, weaving, adding ribbons, glitter and, of course, the most sparkling gems she could find.

The next day Melody rushed off to find Rex to show him what she had made.

'Just watch this, Rex!' she said.
The other mermaids were watching too.

She put on her new shoes and bounced off the sea floor, gliding through the water at full-speed.

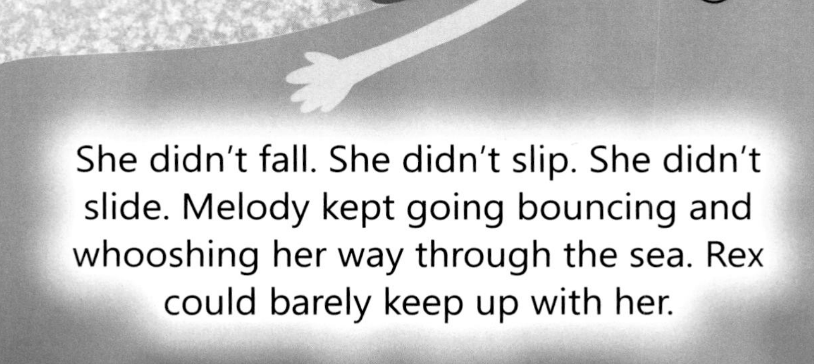

She didn't fall. She didn't slip. She didn't slide. Melody kept going bouncing and whooshing her way through the sea. Rex could barely keep up with her.

"How are you doing it, Melody?" he called, out of breath as he swam after her.

"It's the jellyfish, Rex!" she laughed as she whizzed through the ocean. The jellyfish who were at the tip of her tail grinned too, enjoying the bouncing and the whooshing.

Everyone stopped and stared as she zoomed past them. The other mermaids were filled with awe. They couldn't believe that Melody, the slowest mermaid, had now become the fastest mermaid of them all.

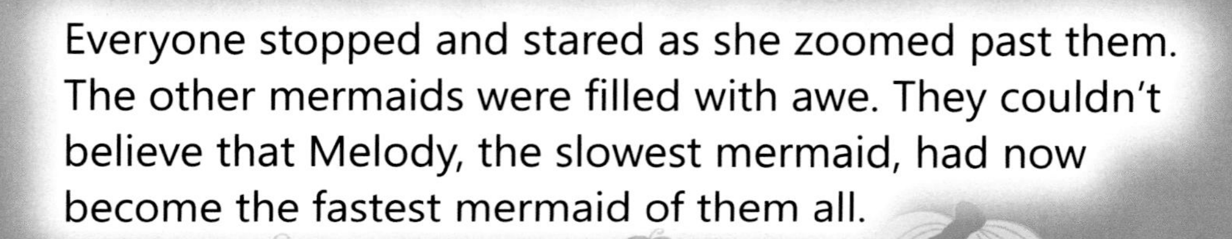

From that day on, Melody was known as the fastest mermaid in the sea! Melody had done it.

All the other mermaids admired her, and they all wanted their own bouncing shoes, so that is exactly what she did...

She opened her
own shop!

Her shop was filled with every type of shoe you could imagine. High, low, strappy, shiny, sporty, boots and, of course, sparkly shoes!

"Hard work really does pay off. I'm proud of you," smiled Rex. "I knew you could do it."
"Not without your support and bouncy tail to give me my idea," Melody smiled back.

This is Melody with her long curly hair, bright blue eyes

and the biggest smile you ***ever*** saw.

About the Author

Mandy has always wanted to write a children's book and now with three young children of her own, it's the perfect time! She loves making games for them to enjoy and sharing a book that sparks their imagination. Family and friends are everything, her books teach children that with good friends and a bit of self belief you can do anything.

Acknowledgements

A special thank you to my husband, Cameron, for being the ultimate support with much needed pep talks and hugs, I wouldn't have got here without you… Team Awesome!

Thank you to Lucy my manager for inspiring me to 'play big' and giving me the confidence to pursue a dream.